CONRAD
THE COLLECTOR

BY

SHARON WOLFE

Conrad The Collector
Copyright © 2019 by Sharon Wolfe

Tellwell Talent
www.tellwell.ca

ISBN
978-0-2288-0293-8 (Hardcover)
978-0-2288-0292-1 (Paperback)

To my beloved grandsons,
Nico and Aidan Ravitch,
whose love of stories
inspired
Conrad's adventures.

And to
Talia, Brandon, Noa and
Nicole Wolfe and the fun we
shared on our four cousin
adventures

TABLE OF CONTENTS

CHAPTER ONE

IN SEARCH OF DRAGON GOD DROPPINGS

Conrad was not an ordinary boy. He didn't like sports. He didn't like video games. He didn't like ice cream, and, most of all, he didn't like messy rooms. He liked reading more than recess, math more than gym. He thought girls were nice, even though most of the boys in his class said they were "yucky."

Some kids thought Conrad was weird, but Conrad didn't care. He liked what he liked. And what he liked most of all was collecting things.

In the beginning, Conrad collected bubble gum wrappers, pieces of string, and rubber bands. In the summer, he collected seashells, and in the fall, he collected coloured leaves. He took stamps off his parents' envelopes and the tops off pop bottles.

When he got older, he became more particular. So particular that the only collections he was really interested in were the ones that took imagination.

"I want my collection to be different than everybody's," Conrad would say.

And he had the imagination to do just that.

Conrad was eight years old when his family moved to Hong Kong. He didn't like leaving his friends in Miami, and he didn't want to move so far away from his granny and grandpa who lived in Montreal, but his dad told him they didn't have a choice.

"When you work for a big bank like I do, you have to go where they send you. We're lucky to be going to Hong Kong. It's one of the world's best cities, and I'm sure you're going to have great fun discovering new and interesting things."

Once Conrad started school and met some of the children living near him in Repulse Bay, he decided his dad was right. It was fun being in a new place. And he was especially pleased to find out that he was an expat. It sounded so adventurous.

I'm a world traveler. I left my home. I crossed the ocean. I'm living in a far-away land. I'm an expat—an expat explorer, Conrad would think to himself.

Many of the families living in Repulse Bay were also expats, which meant they had come from somewhere else and would be staying in Hong Kong for just a while before moving on to another city or country. Most of his neighbours spoke English, even the people who came from Iran or Spain like the El-Mohud and Gormez families.

And best of all, most had children who went to the Hong Kong International School with Conrad.

Conrad's family had moved to Hong Kong around the same time Nico and Aidan's family arrived. The two brothers moved in next door, and the boys became best friends. They enjoyed doing the same things, and what they enjoyed most of all was going on collecting expeditions.

"Conrad is the greatest collector in all of Repulse Bay and maybe in all of Hong Kong," Nico told the kids at school.

What the brothers liked best about going on expeditions with Conrad was that they never knew where his imagination would take them. Often Conrad himself didn't know.

"I just wait for sparks to fly in my brain," he'd tell anyone who asked.

One day, Conrad's sparkly imagination led the brothers on an expedition to the huge apartment building across the street from where they lived.

Conrad had wanted to explore there for some time, ever since his dad had told him the reason why the building looked so strange. And today was the day he had been waiting for.

"The big square hole in the middle of the building is for the Dragon God to pass through," Conrad explained on the way there.

"You've got to be kidding," said Nico.

"I'm just telling you what my dad told me. He said many Chinese people believe in feng shui. I don't really get what that is, but I know it's supposed to have something to do with wind and water and people living with nature."

"But what—" Nico started to ask but stopped himself. It was not like either of the boys to interrupt Conrad when he was discussing his plans. Usually they waited patiently, but usually Conrad didn't talk in riddles.

Nico didn't like riddles. He didn't like that his friends always got the answers faster than he did. And today he knew for sure that he wouldn't be able to figure out what a building with a hole in the middle had to do with wind and water. And what that had to do with the collecting expedition Conrad seemed excited about.

Conrad, realizing that his friends were becoming confused, explained, "My dad said the people living there believe a Dragon God lives in the mountain behind the apartments.

7

The hole is there so it can easily travel from its home behind the building to the sea for its daily bath."

Pointing to the waters of Repulse Bay, Conrad continued, "They're afraid that if the Dragon God gets stuck or lost on its way to the sea, all its good energy will be blocked. That will bring bad luck to everyone who lives inside."

The brothers were having a hard time believing what Conrad was saying.

"That's woowee-poohwee. There's no such thing as a Dragon God," said Nico.

"Woowee-poohwee," echoed Aidan.

Conrad also had his doubts. He knew it would be quite a challenge to find out if the Dragon God was lurking around. And that made it all the more exciting because Conrad loved challenges. It was one of the things he liked best about expeditions.

"There's only one way to know if it's true or not. We have to check it out for ourselves."

Conrad didn't add anything more. He didn't have to. The others knew him well enough to know he was hoping to find something that the Dragon God may have dropped or lost. Anything cool that would be a perfect addition to his collection.

They walked all around the humongous building. Conrad and Nico picked up a few things, studied them, and then dropped them. Aidan didn't join in the search. He didn't want to find anything. Oh no, not this time. He didn't want proof that a Dragon God lived just across the street.

An hour went by. Still nothing. "Can we go home now?" asked Aidan, hoping his brother was getting tired of bending over, searching through grass, weeds, and dirt.

"Not yet. We'll be done soon, Aidan," said Nico, who was also beginning to get tired. Searching without finding anything was no fun. Even Conrad was looking a bit disheartened.

"We can't give up now. We just have to look harder, team. There has to be something somewhere that the Dragon God lost or dropped on its way to the sea."

The brothers didn't argue. They had been on collecting expeditions before, and they knew when Conrad sounded this sure, he was usually right. More time passed. They kept on with their investigation. Still, they found nothing that might have been connected to the Dragon God.

Nothing, that is, until Conrad pushed away a few twigs and picked up a rather strange yet somewhat familiar object. He didn't say a word. He slowly turned it over. He looked at it carefully. Nico and Aidan watched quietly from the distance.

Then, suddenly, Conrad's face broke into a huge I-think-I-discovered-something smile.

"I've got it! This is part of a broken tooth. It's way too big to come from a person, but it could come from some huge kind of animal. And look, it's really yellow, like my mom always says my teeth will get if I don't brush them." Conrad's imagination was sparking off in several directions.

"Team, it's very possible that this tooth fell out of the mouth of the Dragon God. I think it's the proof we've been looking for."

"Fantastico," said Nico, rushing over to have a look. "I knew you'd find something."

"Let's go home. I don't wanna be here when the Dragon God comes looking for his tooth," said Aidan, who was more scared than excited.

Conrad was also ready to leave. It had taken them a long time to find the dragon's tooth, and he couldn't wait to get home and safely stow this precious treasure in his collector's box.

My Fellow Story Lovers:

Sometimes when we're little
and we have a lot to learn
we make mistakes, it happens
even Conrad had a turn.
He always kept it secret
no one did he tell
but in tomorrow's story
you'll share in it as well.

CHAPTER TWO

IT ALL STARTED
WITH ICICLES

Everybody who knew Conrad knew that he was the most unusual, most imaginative collector in all Repulse Bay. So amazing, in fact, that his friends thought he was born that way. They thought because he came from a family of collectors, he always knew everything there was to know about collecting.

But they were wrong. Very wrong. That was not at all the way it was.

Conrad had to learn about collecting just like everybody else. However, his friends couldn't know that, because Conrad never told anyone about the very silly mistake he made many years before when he first tried to put a collection together.

That was his deepest, darkest secret. A secret that only he and Grammy shared. Until now, when you're about to find out.

Oh, it's true, Conrad did come from a family of collectors. His mother collected cookie jars. Many, many cookie jars. So many, in fact, that there were cookie jars in every room of the house. There was even a Minnie Mouse and a fat, jolly baker cookie jar in the bathroom.

Conrad's dad collected fishing lures. Those pretty feathery things fishermen put on their lines to fool the fish into thinking they were about to swallow a juicy bug.

Conrad didn't like to fool fish like that. But he did like it when his dad took out his tackle box and told him all kinds of interesting stuff, like which lures attracted which kinds of fish.

His favourite cousin, Shelby, collected beach glass. But when Conrad asked to see it, Shelby usually wasn't in the mood to show it.

So, with all this collecting going on around him, it was only natural Conrad wanted his very own collection.

That's how his deepest, darkest secret came to be.

When Conrad was four years old and too young to play outside on his own, his only hope of finding something interesting to collect was when he was out and about with his mom or dad. But they were always in a hurry. They never had time to wait while Conrad figured out what he wanted.

But that was about to change.

One day Conrad got news that made his hopes fly sky-high. "Con, how would you like to come with me to visit Grammy and Grandpa in Montreal?" asked his dad.

"For real?" answered Conrad, jumping up and down with excitement.

He was happy because it was the first time he was going on a trip alone with his dad. Happy because he'd never been on an airplane.

And happy most of all because he knew that Grammy didn't rush around like the rest of his family.

"I bet I'll have lots of time to find things when I'm out with Grammy," Conrad told his friend Heather. "My Grammy isn't so fast. She won't tell me to hurry up when I want to look for stuff."

But sadly, that wasn't to be.

When Conrad arrived in Montreal, he got some very sad news. Grammy had fallen down and hurt her hip.

"I'm so sorry, Connie. I'll have to stay indoors while you're here. Still, I'm sure we'll find some fun things to do together," she said.

Conrad's plan for going on a collecting expedition with his Grammy was ruined. He was very disappointed, even though he tried not to let it show.

Fortunately, his disappointment didn't last very long.

It was February, and February in Montreal meant snow. Lots and lots of snow. Conrad had never seen snow before. He and his family were living in Miami at the time. It had never snowed there, so Conrad couldn't wait to go out and play in it.

Better still, Grammy lived on a very quiet street. It had only three houses and hardly any traffic. That meant he could go out all by himself. All he had to do was promise not to cross the road.

"I promise," said Conrad, and off he went.

Conrad loved how white and twinkly the snow was. He loved how cold and fresh it felt.

"This snow stuff is fantastic," Conrad said aloud. He often talked to himself when he was alone. Especially when he was excited.

He walked down the street, picking up little lumps of frozen snow that he carefully placed in his pockets. He broke off tiny icicles that had formed along the neighbour's fence and others that were dangling from frozen bushes. He added every piece to his collection. Conrad was feeling good. Even better than good. He was feeling great.

For sure I'll have the best collection in the family, he thought. The more he thought about it, the happier he became, and the happier he became, the merrier he looked.

Unfortunately, the merry look didn't last for long. It disappeared soon after he arrived back at Grammy's house.

"Connie, you must be a little chilly after such a long walk. Go sit by the fire and I'll bring you a nice hot cup of cocoa," said Grammy.

Conrad settled himself next to the fireplace and watched the colourful flames leaping about. He was enjoying the crackling sound and the smell of the burning wood when suddenly...

He felt something. Something wet was trickling down both his legs.

Wow, this is soooo weird. My legs are leaking, he thought.

Just then Grammy came in with the cocoa. As she came close to Conrad, her kind, sweet smile disappeared.

"Oh, Connie, what have we here?" she asked, spying the puddle on the floor. "I thought you were too old to have this kind of accident. Surely you remember where the bathroom is."

"Grammy, this isn't pee," said Conrad. "My legs are leaking. See? Water's running down from the sides of my legs."

"Don't be silly, Connie," said Grammy. "Legs don't leak. Cartons leak. Pens leak. Pockets leak. Uh-oh. That must be it. Did you put something wet in your pockets?"

"No way, Grammy. The only thing I put in my pockets is my collection."

"And what might you be collecting, young man?" asked Grammy.

"Snow lumps, Grammy. I'm collecting pieces of hard snow so I'll have a collection like everyone else in my family."

"Connie, those snow lumps are called icicles. No one can make a collection out of icicles. Didn't you know that snow melts?" said Grammy, shaking her head.

Conrad hadn't given a thought to whether or not snow melted. After all, he had only arrived in snowy Montreal the day before, and no one, especially a four-year-old, could think of everything in just one day.

Conrad noticed Grammy's smile had returned.

"Off you go, Mr. Collector. There are fresh towels in the bathroom. Dry yourself off and change those pants," she said, shaking her head and smiling once again.

Conrad didn't feel like smiling. He wasn't happy his collection had melted. What made him feel even worse was he had embarrassed himself in front of his Grammy.

Conrad decided to stay in his room until suppertime. And so he did.

He might not have come out even then, except he was getting hungry, and some very delicious smells were drifting up from the kitchen.

Eventually, Conrad went downstairs and took his place at the table. He sat as still as a mouse hiding from the family cat. As he waited for someone to mention his silly mistake, he grew more and more uncomfortable.

Time passed. Still nobody, not Grandpa, not his dad, not even Grammy mentioned anything about what had happened. Dessert came and still not a word was said.

That's when Conrad finally realized that Grammy was keeping it a secret between just the two of them. Conrad always loved Grammy, but that night he loved her more than ever.

And the best was still to come.

Just when Grammy was serving her ever-so-tasty apple pie, Grandpa said, "Con, why don't you and I do some exploring tomorrow? I know lots of interesting places we could visit. You might even be lucky enough to find something you'd like to bring home."

"Can we take our time and just look around for stuff?" asked Conrad.

"What kind of stuff do you have in mind?" asked Grandpa.

"I don't know now, Grandpa, but I'll know what it is when I see it."

"Sounds like a good plan to me."

"Me too," said Conrad as he took a big bite of his apple pie. *Tomorrow, I'll start my collection for real,* he thought happily.

So now you know Conrad's deepest secret. And it all started with icicles.

Fellow Adventurers:

The snow lump collection
happened a time long ago.
The adventures that follow,
as the next stories show,
all happen when Conrad's
much older was he
had become the best of collectors.
Read on and you'll see.

CHAPTER THREE

WHO SAYS GROSS ISNT COOL?

A few weeks after their Dragon God expedition, the boys were about to go exploring when the weather turned cold and nasty. Usually they were disappointed if their plans were ruined. Not this time.

This time, Nico and Aidan were happy to stay indoors because Conrad had promised to show them his latest collection. He had been working on it for some time, but he never showed his collections to anyone, not even his two best friends, until they were put together just the way he wanted them to be.

"Look at this one," said Conrad as he gingerly picked up a large, crinkly, purplish scab.

"Wow. Is it ever huge. How did you get it?" asked Nico.

"Remember when I fell off my bike and cut myself so bad my mother thought I'd need stitches? Well, it's a good thing we didn't go to the hospital, 'cause if they'd stitched me up, I wouldn't have this beauty to add to my collection."

Conrad held up tiny scabs one by one so his friends could examine them more closely. "These little guys here are from when I had chicken pox."

"But you had chicken pox last year. How come the scabs didn't just fall apart?" asked Nico, eyeing the various shaped treasures that Conrad kept removing from an old matchbox.

Nico was a quiet boy with a curious mind and an excellent memory. Because he didn't talk a lot, people thought he was shy, but it wasn't that. He just liked to be very sure of something before he said it aloud. However, that didn't stop him from asking questions. As many questions as his very curious mind could think up.

And the person he questioned most was Conrad. Nico thought that Conrad, besides being a great collector, was also a super-duper adventurer who knew lots of stuff that Nico wanted to know about too.

Conrad liked that Nico asked questions. He liked that Nico would say "fantastico" whenever Conrad told him stuff and took him on adventures. He liked that they never had fights like some of the other boys in their class.

Except, that is, the one big mad-on that occurred soon after they met. Conrad told Nico he was going to the Repulse Bay beach, not far from his home, to hunt for something unusual for his collection. When Nico told his mother where he and Conrad were going to go, she called Conrad's mum to say the boys were too young to go so close to the water by themselves.

Conrad's mother agreed, and Conrad blamed Nico for ruining his plans. But that was a long time ago, and Nico felt so bad about it that Conrad couldn't stay mad at him for long.

"Let me smell them," said Aidan, leaning over the others to take a whiff of the scabs.

"They don't smell, silly. They're too old," Nico said, feeling big and important, as he always did when he could show Conrad that he knew more stuff than his little brother.

"Your brother's right, Aidan. When the scabs get kind of crunchy looking, like these, it means the blood's dried up. No blood. No smell. No smell means no mother coming in my room to find out what's going on."

Nico's just a big show-off, Aidan thought, trying to hide his embarrassment. *He wants Conrad to see how smart he is, but he's not so smart. He's just older, and when I get old, I'll know all that stuff too. Then Nico won't be such a big shot.*

Nico was so excited about seeing Conrad's collection, he hadn't stopped to think that calling his brother silly was hurtful. His mind was too flooded with all the questions that were popping up in his head.

"Is it hard to peel them off? Did you count them? How many are there?" Nico could hardly wait for Conrad to answer one thing before he asked another.

"I have eleven from chicken pox. This big one is from the time I fell off my bike, and I got these two when I tripped over the hose last summer."

The boys just couldn't believe what they were seeing. "Fantastico. I bet no one else in the whole world ever thought of collecting scabs," said Nico.

"Me too. I think that," said Aidan, who didn't want to be left out of the conversation.

"You're probably right," said Conrad, happy that his friends were so impressed. "It does take imagination, and that's my speciality."

Reaching into his matchbox again, he pulled out his favourite scab. "Look at this one. I call it Apple."

"You give your scabs names?" exclaimed Aidan, his eyes wide with surprise.

"Naw. Just this one. It looks a lot like the apple on my mom's computer."

The brothers nodded. They were having such a good time just letting their imaginations follow Conrad's lead.

"I don't remember how I got the rest, but they're all from me. That's for sure," exclaimed Conrad as he ever so carefully returned his precious collection back to its resting place.

Then, as the boys watched quietly, he wrapped the tiny box in a towel and placed it back underneath his bed.

"My mother better not find these," he said. "You know how girls are. She'd think they were gross and make me throw them away. No way can I let that happen. This is my best collection yet."

"Awesome," said Nico, who thought his friend was the coolest person he'd ever met. "There can't be another collection as fantastico as this."

Dear Fellow Adventurers:

Many of Conrad's collections

don't come close

to that one which was really gross.

But since that one has now been read,

tomorrow before you go to bed,

follow along with our adventurous boy

on a treasure hunt you're sure to enjoy.

CHAPTER FOUR

PIRATES
OF REPULSE BAY

Conrad could sense when it was time to go on a collecting expedition. A restless feeling would creep over him. It began in his foot, which started tap-tapping on the floor. Then it would move slowly up the rest of his body until he couldn't get comfortable, no matter where or how he sat.

Experience had taught him the only way to shake off that uncomfortable twitchy feeling was to concentrate on something new to collect. And so he did. He thought and he thought.

Finally, Conrad had a plan. A plan he eagerly shared with Nico and Aidan. Repulse Bay, where they lived, was on the most sheltered side of Hong Kong Island. Hundreds of years ago, pirates were said to have come to hide out, bury their treasures, and plan their future exploits there.

Conrad had no idea where the pirates went or where they might have hidden their treasure once they landed. But he had a hunch this was the day he was going to find out.

He gathered up the equipment he needed for the expedition. He took out his magnifying glass, flashlight, and poking stick. He also got his rubber boots and his favourite collection bag, the one with a very sturdy handle.

Most collectors wouldn't think to take a flashlight and rubber boots on a beautiful sunny day. But Conrad, as you know, was not like most collectors. He had a most vivid imagination.

And today his imagination told him that when he was out searching for pirate things for his collection, it might be smart to check out all the rocky places that stretched from the beach down along the boardwalk and up to the end point of the shoreline.

"Imagine if I found a pirate's cave, and I couldn't see where the treasure was buried because I didn't have a flashlight," said Conrad as he struggled to pull on his rubber boots.

Putting on his boots was difficult for Conrad. Although he didn't want people to know, he still had a lot of trouble telling which boot went on which foot. When he forced the wrong one on the wrong foot, well, then he had to tug and tug to remove it. But he felt he had no choice. All the pirates he had ever seen in books wore big, black boots, so Conrad figured he should do the same.

"Let's get a move on, mates," he called out.

His friends needed no urging. They could hardly contain their excitement. Off they ran. Minutes later, they arrived at the beach.

While Conrad was carefully planning their first move, Aidan and Nico, who were also excellent spotters, began to look around.

Suddenly, Aidan shrieked in delight, "Hey, guys, look at this." He had found an absolutely perfectly formed conch shell.

"It's a beauty," said Nico.

"It's okay," said Conrad, hardly looking at it. "But that's not what we're here to collect. We're looking for pirate's treasure."

Conrad was usually more considerate of Aidan's feelings. He knew that he was two years younger and sometimes had a hard time keeping up. But at that moment Conrad was on a quest, and sometimes when his mind was so wrapped up in his quest he could think of nothing else.

"So what if it's not pirate stuff?" said Aidan. "It's a treasure from the sea, and I'm collecting it anyways." He slipped it gently into his pocket.

Suddenly, Conrad felt a familiar feeling. Not like the restless feeling that told him that it was time to go collecting. No, this was a bubbling-up kind of feeling, one that usually came when something adventurous was about to happen.

He closed his eyes and concentrated very hard. So hard that he held his breath. So hard he didn't even realize he wasn't breathing.

"Over there, team. Head for the mountain over there."

The words were barely out of Conrad's mouth when they started running straight for the rocks that jutted out of the sea and formed a large wall along the shoreline.

The interesting thing was that the boys had often played all kinds of games on those rocks before. Sometimes they imagined they were knights, and the rocks were the king's castle. Sometimes they pretended to be Pokémon characters hiding out from their trainers. Sometimes they even imagined they were wild horses running free through the fields and mountains of Asia. That was Aidan's favourite game.

But they had never seen a cave. And they never, ever found anything that made them think pirates had been there.

So although Aidan and Nico ran fast to catch up to Conrad, deep down they were wondering why he was so excited. What did he expect to find at this place they had been to so many times before?

Conrad wasn't at the rocks for more than a minute or two when he suddenly gasped and squatted down. Nico and Aidan watched silently from a little distance away. They knew that Conrad didn't like to be disturbed when he was in the middle of a discovery.

Just when they couldn't stand the suspense one moment longer, Conrad said in almost a whisper, "Mates, I think not so long ago there were visitors to these rocks. Look at this."

Aidan and Nico, eager to see what Conrad had discovered, rushed over and looked to where he was pointing. In front of them was a pile of smoking ashes left from a recent bonfire, a few sticks with their tips burned off, and a wrapper from a package of hotdogs that had been torn up and tossed between some of the smaller stones.

"D-d-do you think pirates were here last night?" stuttered Aidan.

"Could be," answered Conrad.

Nico shook his head. "No way. I've seen lots of pictures of pirates in my books, and I never, ever saw a picture of a pirate eating a hot dog."

"What do they eat then?" asked Conrad.

Nico thought for a moment. "I'm not sure. Could be they roast their old parrots."

"That's mean," said Aidan.

Conrad picked up one of the sticks and pushed it around in the ashes. Suddenly he spied something white and small and pointy. Quickly, he pulled the magnifying glass out of his back pocket. The boys bent down to have a closer look. It was a bone, a tiny white bone.

"It's a bone from a parrot," Conrad exclaimed.

"Nix-nix chopsticks. It looks like a chicken bone to me, "said Nico, whose thinking had not yet caught up with his friend's imagination.

"Nix-nix chopsticks," said Aidan, siding with his big brother.

"Sorry mates. You're wrong," said Conrad. "That's no chicken bone. It's from a parrot. It's proof that someone was here last night and roasted a parrot."

A quiet hush fell over the group. For a few moments, no one moved. Then, gently and ever so carefully, Conrad reached down and picked up the bone. His heart was pounding with excitement as he slipped it into his collector's bag.

"D-d-do you think the pirates are hiding somewhere near these rocks?" asked Aidan, trying to sound braver than he felt.

"I bet they are. I bet their cave is right up in that mountain over there," said Conrad.

The boys' eyes followed his pointing finger. They knew the huge pile of rocks leaning against the hillside at the farthest edge of the shoreline was not high enough to be called a mountain. But they also knew the fun they always had when they went along with Conrad's imagination. They were quick to agree.

"Yeah, that's it. That must be a pirate mountain."

Nico and Conrad raced along the beach toward the rocky mountain. Aidan hung back for a bit. He wasn't so sure that he wanted to find the pirate's treasure, especially if it meant the pirates might be lurking some-where nearby.

"What if they're sleeping in a cave and we wake them up?" Aidan asked.

The older boys, paying no attention to him, scurried up the rocks. They poked their sticks in between the large stones. Minutes passed. They were about to give up all hope of finding anything when Conrad spied the narrow crack almost hidden between two large boulders. Could it be? It sure looked like...

"Hey, mates, look at this!" Conrad called out. "It's the cave we've been searching for."

As quick as could be, Conrad disappeared through the crack in the rocks. Nico and Aidan could see the beam of his flashlight. Aidan could no longer pretend to be brave.

"Nico, I-I-I don't want to go in there. Stay with me," he pleaded.

Before Nico had a chance to reply, Conrad reappeared with the biggest smile on his face.

"Di-did you find buried treasure?" Aidan asked, so excited that he almost forgot to be scared.

"No, I didn't find it, but I found something just as good," declared Conrad. "Look at this."

He opened his hand slowly. The brothers gasped. Conrad was holding something shaped like a triangle. It was black. Even though it was very old and very dirty, it certainly looked as if it could have been shiny at one time.

"Do you know what I think this is?" began Conrad.

Nico shrieked, "I know. I know. It's a pirate's eyepatch."

"Righto-dynamio," said Conrad. "It's definitely an eyepatch."

While Conrad and Aidan were carefully examining their latest find, Nico went off to do some exploring on his own. Suddenly he found something that made his heart jump.

It was a very large, very wide piece of wood. Although it was rickety and broken, it resembled something Nico had seen many times in his pirate picture books.

This looks like the planks the pirates forced people to walk on! He thought.

He hesitated before he called out to the others, because if there was one thing Nico didn't like to do, it was to make a silly mistake.

He examined the board carefully. He turned it from one side to the other. He closed his eyes and tried to picture what he had seen in his books.

I bet this was really strong before it got all old and broken up, thought Nico.

When he felt as sure as he could feel, he called out, "Hey, Conrad, Aidan, look what I found."

Since Conrad was certain that nothing anyone discovered could be as super-great as the parrot bone and pirate's eyepatch, he took his time, carefully putting the patch into his collector's bag before heading off in the direction of Nico's voice. He got there in time to see Nico and Aidan jumping up and down with excitement.

Conrad took one look at what Nico was holding, and his mouth dropped. "Is it? Do you think...?"

"Yep. It's gotta be a plank from a pirate ship," Nico said, now quite sure of himself.

"Way to go, mate," said Conrad.

Nico was as proud as proud could be. He had found something great to add to Conrad's collection. And he had found it all by himself.

What made him even happier, if that was possible, was that Conrad, who often shared stuff he found with his best friends, said, "If it's okay with Nico, who discovered this great find, why don't we each break off a piece of the plank for our very own collections."

On the way home, the boys couldn't stop talking about how lucky they had been.

"What a fantastic day this has turned out to be," said Conrad. "We found a parrot's bone, an eyepatch, and a plank from a pirate's ship."

This has to be the absolutely positively, best collecting day ever," said Nico.

"So far," said Conrad. "We never know what we can find next time."

Aidan, walking beside Nico and Conrad, thinking of the beautiful conch shell in his pocket, agreed.

To all of you with your fun imaginations:

Conrad's imagined a perfect gift
but it wasn't as easy as it did seem
something he didn't figure on
threatened to ruin his scheme.
The next chapter tells that tale
explains what it's about.
Will imagination win the day?
Or will our hero just
Strike out?

CHAPTER FIVE

THE DELICIOUS DILEMMA

It was Aidan's birthday. Conrad really liked birthdays, and he really liked Aidan. So it was a bit surprising when he awoke that he didn't just pop up and start getting dressed immediately. Instead, lost in thought, he remained seated at the edge of the bed. It was his mother calling out to ask what was taking him so long that finally snapped Conrad into action.

"Good morning, Connie. You look like something's bothering you. What's up?" his mother asked as she watched him stir the cereal round and round in his bowl.

"I'm just thinking, that's all. Today's Aidan's party. I want to give him something great, but I can't think of anything special enough."

"We can go shopping after breakfast, and you can pick out whatever you think he'd like," said his mother.

"I can't do that. Aidan would be so disappointed. He knows I'm an honest-to-goodness collector, and honest-to-goodness collectors never go to a store and buy something."

Conrad got up from the table. "I'm going to look through my collections. Maybe I'll think of something," he said and left the room.

Conrad took out boxes from his cupboard and the scab collection from under the bed. He looked and he thought. He thought and he looked.

"Nothing's coming. Think, Conrad, think," he muttered to himself as he reached into yet another box. Out fell a cookie crumb.

"This must have been from when we were playing the other day. Aidan sure loved Mom's cookies." Conrad jumped to his feet, shrieking. "I got it. I'll give him a collection of cookies. He'll love it. For sure it'll be the best present ever."

Conrad had never collected cookies before, but even so, he knew he wouldn't need his magnifying glass, flashlight, poking stick, and rubber boots this time.

"I just need something to put them in," he told his mother.

Bags in hand, off he went. Conrad hadn't walked far before he smelled a wonderful aroma coming from Mrs. Porgy's house.

Conrad followed the delicious smell around to the back of the house and called in through her open window, "Hi, Mrs. Porgy. It's me, Conrad."

"Well hello, Conrad, and what would you be collecting today, might I ask?" Everyone in the neighbourhood knew how much Conrad enjoyed collecting things.

"It's a special collection, Mrs. Porgy. I'm collecting cookies. Different kinds of cookies, and they have to be really good because I'm giving them to my best friend Aidan,for his birthday."

"Your friend Aidan sure picked a good time to have a birthday. It's close to the holidays, and people living here come from so many places. I bet you'll be getting a lot of very interesting cookies to give to your friend.

"That's super great, Mrs. Porgy, because I'll need to get more than one kind. I need hundreds of kinds," Conrad explained.

"Well, I'm not sure that you'll get hundreds of kinds of cookies around here, but to help you get started, I'll give you two gingerbread cookies. How's that, Mr. Collector?"

The cookies smelled so good, and Conrad wanted them so much, but something he hadn't planned for had just happened. And now he had a problem. A huge problem.

Conrad's mother had told him that he must never be greedy. She had taught him if someone gave him something, he was to say, "Thank you very much."

He knew it would be rude to ask Mrs. Porgy to give him another one. Conrad put the two cookies into the bag carefully, thanked Mrs. Porgy, and off he went.

As he walked down the path, he grumbled to himself, "Two cookies won't be enough. Aidan needs a great collection because it's his birthday. If I give a collection to Aidan and keep a collection of my own, there won't be any for Nico. Nico will feel bad. Then Aidan would feel bad if he sees Nico's sad. And I'll feel terrible if I made my best friends sad. My whole plan could be ruined."

Suddenly he thought of something that cheered him up. Mrs. Porgy was right. It was Chanukah and almost Christmas. Everybody would be baking holiday cookies. For sure he'd get another gingerbread man. Then he'd have three, and they could each have one for their collections.

Walking along, he smelled another really good smell. The smell led him right to Mrs. Greenbaum's wide-open kitchen window. "Hi, Mrs. Greenbaum, those cookies sure smell terrific," he said.

"Well, if it isn't Conrad the Collector himself." Conrad loved it when people called him that. It made him feel proud and kind of grown up.

"And what are you collecting today?" asked Mrs. Greenbaum.

"Cookies," he said. "I want to give my friend a cookie collection for his birthday."

"What a generous boy you are," said Mrs. Greenbaum. "Here are two dreidel cookies for your collection."

Conrad really liked Mrs. Greenbaum. He really liked that the dreidel cookies looked like toy tops. But he wasn't happy. One dreidel cookie had to be for Aidan, and if he gave the other to Nico, he wouldn't have a dreidel cookie for his own collection.

"Maybe someone else is baking Chanukah cookies, and then I can get another dreidel one," he said hopefully.

As he approached Mrs. Chang's house, Conrad once again smelled a wonderful smell. *This is it! Now I'll get that extra gingerbread man*, he thought.

But no, Mrs. Chang gave Conrad two Chinese moon cookies. "Conrad, if your friend likes Oreo cookies, I think he's going to like these even more," she said as she handed Conrad two round sandwich-shaped cookies. "Instead of white icing, these have a lotus seed paste filling."

Conrad, always polite, was sure to thank Mrs. Chang, but as he went down the walk, he muttered softly to himself, "I'm not so sure Aidan will think lotus seed tastes better than Oreo icing."

Mrs. Mohamed was next. She had just taken baklava out of the oven. "You be sure to tell the birthday boy that these are delicious, even if they don't look like cookies usually do. My mother taught me how to make them when I was a little girl in Lebanon. They have honey, sugar, nuts, and chocolate pieces," she said as she handed two pieces of delicious smelling baklava to Conrad.

Conrad studied the two pieces for a moment. "Thank you, Mrs. Mohamed. These cookies have a really interesting shape. They'll be great in the collection."

On his next stop he had a really nice chat with Ankasa, a classmate who explained that that very day was Bodi Day and to celebrate it

Buddhists bake heart-shaped cookies to look like the leaves of the Bodi tree.

"We have brought most of our cookies to the temple, but there are some left over. One minute and I'll get some for you."

"Some" sounded good to Conrad. Some was more than two, or so he thought until Ankasa returned with two pretty little hearts.

"These look really nice. Thanks, Ankasa. See you tomorrow." said Conrad, hiding his disappointment.

And so it went.

Conrad spoke with every neighbour who was at home. Each person was happy to give him cookies, which had been made from their very own back-at-home holiday recipes. Soon the most wonderful smells were coming from the bags Conrad gently carried from house to house.

When there were no more houses to go to, Conrad went home, opened his collection bags, took out all the cookies he had received, and spread them out on the kitchen table. They looked so different. So very tasty ... even the ones that didn't look anything like cookies he had ever seen before.

Aidan will really like the Scottish drummer boy shortbreads that Mr. Deans, Robbie's dad made, thought Conrad. *And since Nico loves green tea ice cream, I'll bet his favourite will be the green tea meringues Ms. Hayashi gave me.*

The ones Conrad liked best were the oval cookies with the beautiful angel icing design that Señora Costa had made to celebrate the Mexican holiday, Fiesta of Our Lady of Guadalupe, but he figured he'd never get the chance to taste those.

When his mother came home from shopping, she was surprised to find that her son wasn't looking at all like the very-pleased-with-himself boy she had been expecting to see.

"Why the glum face, Connie? Did something go wrong with your plan?

"It doesn't work. That's what went wrong. It's my biggest collection ever, and it doesn't work," Conrad answered, looking down at his shoes, something he did only when he was really upset.

"What do you mean? Didn't you get any cookies?"

"I got lots of cookies. Everywhere I went people gave me two. But there are three of us. So I'm stuck. Aidan gets a collection for his birthday. That leaves just one more. If I break it up and give some to Nico and keep some for myself, I won't be an honest-to-goodness collector, because every honest-to-goodness collector knows a collection is not complete if it has missing parts," Conrad explained.

He sat silently for a while, trying to come up with a plan.

Suddenly he jumped up. "I got it! I know what I'm going to do," he said and ran out of the kitchen to get what he needed.

Once everything was in place, he settled down and read his library book until it was time for him to get ready for the party.

The moment he heard his dad arrive home, as quick as a mosquito avoiding a swat, he picked up his cookie gifts and raced out to the car.

When he got to the party, he didn't put his present in the pile with the other gifts. He knew his would be the best, so he wanted Aidan to open it last. Conrad waited until everyone went home. Only then did he hand Aidan the large bag of goodies.

Aidan removed each cookie carefully. "Yippee-coyote! This is awesome. Thanks, thanks so much."

"I knew you'd like it," Conrad said happily. "But wait, there's something else." He went back to where he had hidden the presents.

With a huge smile, he handed Nico the other cookie collection. "This is for you, Nico."

Although Nico was very excited to get a cookie collection of his own, he was afraid Conrad had made a mistake. He hadn't kept anything for himself!

"But it's not my birthday," Nico said quietly. He was almost afraid to be so honest, because he didn't want Conrad to change his mind and take the collection back.

"I know that, silly," said Conrad, "but you're my friend, and I can't be happy unless both my friends are happy. Anyway, I have lots of collections, and I really had fun collecting these," he added, remembering how many of the bakers had referred to him as Conrad the Collector.

"I'm going to save my collection under the bed," said Aidan.

"You can't. You gotta eat it," Nico said. "It's food. If we don't eat it, ants will find it, and it'll be gone-zo."

"But we're supposed to save collections. How can I save it if I've got to eat it?" said Aidan, sounding like he was about to cry.

"You're a hundred percent right, Aidan. Collections are meant to be saved. For sure I've saved all of mine." Conrad said.

Well, almost all of them, he thought, remembering the frozen icicles he had tried to collect when he was little.

Of course, Conrad knew that a cookie collection couldn't last forever. He had already figured out just how disappointed Aidan would be if his very first collection were to disappear because he had to eat it up. No way would Conrad want to give Aidan a collection that disappointed him in the end. It was a dilemma for sure, but Conrad wasn't one to let a dilemma like that defeat him.

"Don't worry. I figured out how you can keep your collection and eat it at the same time," Conrad told his little pal.

"How? Tell me," begged Aidan, excited and happy again.

Conrad went to get a third bag, the one he had hidden away under his coat. Back he came with a huge grin.

"Here's the solution, team," he said as he pulled a camera from the bag. "Just take pictures of your collection to keep, and after that you can eat it."

"Perfecto. You're really good at thinking up stuff, Conrad," said Aidan.

"I'll get something to put the cookies on," said Nico as he ran to the cupboard where his mother kept the bed sheets. He came back with a plain white one.

"Good pick," said Conrad. "The cookies will look super on this."

The boys spread the sheet out and carefully began to arrange the cookies. They matched up the shapes as best they could. The dreidel cookies went next to the Christmas trees, because they both had pointed tops. The Santa Claus cookies looked fine next to the Scottish drummer boys. The boys thought the two Bible-baby cookies, baby Jesus and the baby lambs, looked great side by side, right above the Chinese moon cookies, which they had placed next to the hearts. The green tea meringues were round like the sugar cookies, so they were good together. Nothing looked quite like the stars, so the boys decided to put them beside the Mexican angels because they both lived in the heavens. Just the baklava didn't have a partner, but that was okay.

Conrad handed Aidan the camera so he could take a photo of his very first collection. "This is the coolest birthday gift ever. Thank you, thank you, Conrad. You're my bestest friend," said Aidan.

"I want to take a picture for my collection, too," said Nico. "And Conrad, you've got to take a picture to keep. You collected it, so even if you gave it to us, it still counts as your collection too."

And so it was that three very happy boys took pictures. Many pictures, actually. And when they were finished, the three "bestest" friends sat down to enjoy the most delicious collection ever.

Hang on to your hats, Fellow Adventurers:

A worry bug bites Conrad.

It gives him quite a scare.

He knows he has to face it

although he doesn't dare.

Don't let this confuse you

hang in and you will see

tomorrow night's episode

will answer it perfectly.

CHAPTER SIX

THE COLLECTION
THAT WASNT

Conrad woke one morning and instead of jumping out of bed as usual, he turned on his side, pulled up the covers, and just lay there. And that was very weird behaviour for Conrad, because usually when he woke up he was happy, excited that a new day and possibly a new collecting adventure was about to begin.

But today was not an ordinary day. Oh, no. It was the day when the class was permitted to bring their Pokémon card collections for show-and-tell.

All the boys and girls were very happy because they loved to look at each other's Pokémon cards, but on normal days they were not allowed to bring them to school.

So while all the children in Conrad's class were in a rush to get ready, while everyone was checking their cards to make sure they were in their right places in their binders, Conrad lay still in his bed, his arms folded under his head, looking up at the ceiling.

This was indeed very strange behaviour for Conrad.

"Connie," said his mother, looking into his room, "what are you doing still in bed? It's almost eight. Get up quickly or you'll be late for school."

"I'm not going to school today," Conrad replied.

"Not going to school? Why, you love school. What's wrong? Are you feeling sick? Does something hurt? Maybe I should I call Dr. Hossinfinger."

"No, Mommy. I'm not sick, and nothing hurts, and I don't want to see Dr. Hossinfinger or anyone else. I just want to stay in bed. Please go away. I don't want to talk about it."

Conrad did something he never usually did. He turned on his side so that his back was to his mother, and he pulled the covers right up over his head.

"Connie, talk to me. I know you like school. I know you like collecting. So why wouldn't you, of all people, want to go to school when today is the special Pokémon collector's day? This doesn't make any sense."

"I know you don't get it, but I don't want to talk about it. Please just go away, and let me stay in bed."

Conrad started to cry. Huge sobs. His shoulders shook, and large tears splashed down his cheeks. Soon his top sheet was soggy.

His mother went over to his bed and put her arms around him. She was really beginning to worry.

They sat like that for some time. Slowly, Conrad's big, huge, gulpy sobs got smaller. He felt good in his mother's arms. It was cozy and safe. He was beginning to feel a bit better.

"I can't go," he whispered. "They'll laugh at me if I go."

"Who'll laugh, Connie?"

"Jordon for sure. He'll call me a rice bucket"

"A rice bucket! What's that supposed to mean?" asked his mom.

"It's someone who can eat but can't do anything else. Someone who's useless."

"Oh Conrad, don't you remember what we've talked about? No one, not Jordon, not anyone, can make you feel bad about yourself unless you let them get to you. You know who you are, and someone calling you names can't change that. You'll still be you, Conrad, Repulse Bay's most famous collector."

"You don't get it. The kids will all have better collections than me. They'll say 'Conrad just thinks he's the best collector, but we did better than him.' That's what they'll say, and they'll be right."

With that Conrad pushed himself out of his mother's arms and hid under the blanket again.

"Connie, this is ridiculous. No one has ever laughed at your collections. My goodness, people are always saying what a great collector you are. And anyone who doesn't know that just has to come to your room to see for themselves. Laugh indeed. No one laughs at the collections of Conrad the Collector."

"You're wrong. You don't know anything," screamed Conrad from under the blanket.

"Conrad, there's no need to be rude. I know you're upset, but being rude to the person who's trying to help never makes things better. Now get up and get dressed, because you are going to school."

Conrad peeked out from under the covers and up at his mother. His eyes were rabbit-eye-red, and his nose was all runny. He didn't resemble an adventurous collector. Instead, he looked like a very sad, very scared little boy. A boy who wanted his mommy to help make everything right but who knew in his heart of hearts that she couldn't. He knew that, just as he knew that he had to go to school, whether he wanted to or not.

And so he got out of bed. He washed his face. He got dressed. He ate a tiny bit of breakfast, because he didn't feel at all hungry. When he was about to leave, his mother came to the door and handed him his Pokémon collector's binder.

He didn't want to take it, but he was too sad to argue. He stuffed it down, deep into his schoolbag and walked down the path to wait for the school bus.

That morning, the math lesson seemed to go on and on and on. Then came science, and Conrad thought it would never end. Usually, science was his favourite subject. He loved learning about the environment. Sometimes he got ideas for his collections from the nature lessons. But today the class seemed so long, and he was getting more and more upset, knowing what was about to come next.

Finally, he heard the dreaded words. "It's time for show-and-tell. Everyone take out your Pokémon cards," announced Miss Swandive.

There was an excited buzz in the classroom as everyone took out their Pokémon collections. Hands started to wave. "Can I go first? Please, Miss Swandive," called Andy Shecter.

"No, me, please. Can I go first?" asked Rory.

Only Conrad sat silently looking down, wishing to be anywhere but in that class. Each child had a turn. Some had many cards in their collection. Santiago had the most cards of all. Yoshi had the most duplicates.

Nico had the most shiny cards. Even though Aidan wasn't in their class, Nico knew that his brother had a better collection than anyone. He couldn't wait to go home and tell him.

Show-and-tell was almost over. "Is there anyone who hasn't had a turn?" asked Miss Swandive. No one answered.

Conrad stayed very quiet. He was hardly breathing. He was hoping nobody would notice him.

But Nico did. He looked over to where Conrad was sitting. Conrad was slouched down in his seat. His head was bent forward, and he looked like he wanted to disappear under the desk. Nico could see Conrad didn't want a turn. He sure hoped no one else would catch on.

But that wasn't to be because Sophia had noticed too. Conrad had once shown her parts of his collections, and she thought it was so incredible she couldn't wait to see this one. Sophia was sure as sure as could be that Conrad would have the most and the hardest to get cards of all. Actually, everybody thought that, and that was exactly what Conrad was afraid of.

"We didn't see Conrad's collection, Miss Swandive," called Sophia.

Everyone turned to look at Conrad. "Yeah, it's Conrad's turn," piped in a few of the others.

Conrad could feel everyone's eyes upon him. He could feel his heart beating faster and faster. His face was hot. His hands were clammy. *I don't want to do this*, he thought. But he knew there was no way out. He got up, picked up his Pokémon binder, and walked slowly to the front of the classroom.

"Now let's see what our famous collector has to show us today," said Miss Swandive with a big smile.

Conrad slowly opened his binder, turned it to face his classmates and held it up. There was a huge gasp. No one could believe what they were seeing.

"Turn the page. Turn the page," the kids yelled.

Conrad turned the page. Another gasp.

"It's not possible," said Eduardo.

"Turn another page," said Marie Josie.

But turning the pages didn't make any difference. For no matter how many pages Conrad turned, the result was always the same. They were empty!

Conrad had only collected two cards. He had a Blastoise and a Charmander. And that was that.

The class was shocked. Even the teacher was surprised. And Nico, Conrad's very best friend, got a funny letdown kind of feeling. Although he wasn't sure if he felt letdown for Conrad or for himself.

Conrad didn't say a word. He simply stood there waiting for the laughter he was sure would start at any moment. Waiting for someone to tease him, to call him rice bucket, or Conrad the No-Card Collector.

But no one laughed. No one even thought of teasing him. They were too busy trying to figure out why the best collector they knew had collected only two Pokémon cards.

Hiro broke the silence. "Don't you like Pokémon cards, Conrad?"

"Sure I do," Conrad said so quietly, it was almost a whisper. "I think they're really cool."

"Then how come you only have two?" asked Ivan.

"It's, it's complicated," mumbled Conrad. He was still looking down at the floor, wishing he was anywhere but standing in front of the class.

Nico could see how upset his friend was. He knew that he had to help him. But how? He took a deep breath. "I think I know why Conrad has only collected two Pokémon cards," he said, his voice kind of shaky.

Everyone turned eagerly to look at Nico. Oh, how he wished they'd look somewhere else. Anywhere else. Nico was rather shy and having all those eyes on him was making him very uncomfortable. Still, Conrad needed him. He couldn't worry about being shy now.

So, taking an even deeper breath, Nico continued, "I think Conrad only collects what his imagination tells him to collect," he said, thinking of all the adventures that he and Aidan had on collecting expeditions with Conrad. "His imagination didn't tell him to collect Pokémon cards. Maybe Pokémon cards are boring to Conrad's imagination. Am I right, Conrad?"

Conrad lifted his eyes from the floor and looked at his friend. He had liked Nico for a very long time, since they were in first grade together. He especially liked him when they went on collecting adventures, and he liked him even more at that very moment than he ever did before.

"That's right, Nico." Feeling more like his confident self again Conrad looked around at his classmates, "To me collecting is different. I get an idea. It's like puzzle pieces come into my head. That makes me all excited, like kind of jumpy inside. All I want to do is get my collecting stuff together and go out on a hunt. I just never got that feeling with Pokémon cards. I like them, but I never wanted to hunt them down."

Suddenly, Conrad felt a twinge in the pit of his stomach. His fear had returned.

He took a deep breath before saying. "I guess you'll all think I'm a phony-baloney collector 'cause I don't have any Pokémon cards."

"Nix-nix chopsticks," said Eduardo and Danielle together.

"You have the best collections ever," Nico added, remembering the roasted parrot bone and the cookies and even those gross chicken pox scabs that Conrad kept hidden away in a matchbox under his bed.

"Conrad, it doesn't matter what a person collects. What makes someone a collector is perseverance," said Miss Swandive. "Perseverance means the person is willing to look and look and wait and wait until they find a perfect thing to add to their collection. Everyone knows that you are a real collector with great perseverance, as well as a wonderful imagination."

Miss Swandive's words made Conrad feel happy all over. The class was relieved to see Conrad looking more like himself self again.

They felt even better when Miss Swandive continued, "This class has many excellent collectors. I can tell from what I saw today that everyone worked very hard on their Pokémon card collections. You all had to look and wait a very long time for those missing cards, so you've certainly shown perseverance. You should all be feeling very proud of yourselves."

Suddenly, Nico had an idea. He thought of what he and Aidan often did to build their own Pokémon collections.

"I have an idea, Miss Swandive," he said in a loud voice, not a very, very loud voice, but loud for Nico, who wasn't feeling shy anymore.

"When we get tired of doing our per-seve-rance, we could trade cards. Like, I could trade some of my duplicates."

"Which ones?" asked Ivan.

"I have two shiny Bulbasaur," said Nico, who knew Aidan had a Bulbasaur also, so he didn't mind trading one away. "I'll give you one for a Poliwag."

"I haven't got any shinys," said Stephen.

"I'll trade you a shiny for a Poliwag," said Nico.

The kids loved that idea, and so did Miss Swandive. She told the class they could trade cards for the rest of the afternoon.

Then something especially, unusually, wonderful happened. While all the children were busy talking and trading cards, Nico, remembering how generous Conrad had been to him at Aidan's birthday when he gave him all the cookies, walked over to Conrad, who was standing off to the side, quietly watching everyone. Nico gave him four of his very best duplicates.

Seeing that, Yoshi went over to Conrad. "I have the most duplicates of everybody in the whole class. I don't need so many," he said, handing some of his duplicates to Conrad.

"Here, take these," said Ankasa, giving Conrad two very hard-to-get cards.

Laara was next and others followed. No one had asked the children to do this. No one had to, because over the years Conrad had often shared extra bits of his collections with his classmates.

He had even taken some of the kids on his expeditions, although he did prefer to go mostly with his best friends, Nico and Aidan. Now it was the children's turn to share with Conrad and share they did until

Conrad had a very respectable collection of Pokemon cards.

And so it was that Conrad the Collector's saddest, most scary day turned out to be a very happy day after all.

**Some things are
harder to collect
Then first they seem to be
especially when they're
from Outer Space.
Read tomorrow's chapter
and you'll see.**

CHAPTER SEVEN

THE ALIENS AND THE EARTHLINGS

Conrad was about to enter the kitchen when he overheard his mother saying, "I know it sounds impossible, but lots of people claim they saw it."

"Saw what, Mom?" asked Conrad, whose hearing was almost as sharp as his eyes.

"Nothing, Connie. Just some silly people letting their imaginations run away with them."

"Whose imagination's running where? What are you talking about?" asked Conrad, really excited that his mother was talking about imagination.

"You might as well tell him," said his dad. "You know, Con. He's like a dog with a bone. He won't let go until he hears what it's about."

"Yep, that's me, a dog with a bone. Come on. Please tell me what happened."

"Well, Connie. At the Peak last night, some people saw a strange light in the sky. They were sure it wasn't from a plane and so they—"

In his excitement, Conrad interrupted before his dad had a chance to finish what he was going to say, "They saw an alien spaceship!"

"Hold on, Con. It wasn't a spaceship. Chances are it was either a comet or a meteor," said his dad.

"Or an alien spaceship. It could be that too. There's gotta be a way to find out," said Conrad, his imagination all fired up. "Maybe some pieces fell to earth."

The top of the highest mountain in Hong Kong is called Victoria's Peak. The biggest and most expensive houses are up there. So is Hong Kong International School, which Conrad attended.

Conrad couldn't wait to get to class that morning. He just had to hear what the other parents had told their kids. He wanted to know if any of the adults suggested that it might have been a UFO.

He was in such a hurry to eat breakfast, he poured orange juice instead of milk into his cereal. He was in such a hurry to brush his teeth, he squirted his mother's hand cream onto his toothbrush. And in his rush to get dressed, he put a blue sock on his left foot and his green sock from yesterday on the right foot. But it wasn't gym day, so he didn't think anyone would notice.

Mr. Daniels, Nico and Aidan's dad who was driving carpool that day, had barely pulled to a stop when Conrad jumped in the car to tell his friends the latest news.

"You'll never believe this. Last night, some people on the Peak saw an alien spaceship. It was probably just over our school."

"Cool. A UFO over the school," said Nico, picking up on his friend's excitement. "I wish I'd seen it."

"I don't want a UFO on top of our school. What if there are aliens inside? What if they're coming to do tests on us like they said they do in your book, Nico?" Aidan asked, his voice shaking with fear.

"Don't worry, Aidan," said Nico. "Those aliens won't be doing any tests on us. They probably just flew by to see what life's like here on Earth. Anyway, they're gone now, so we missed everything."

"Maybe not everything," suggested Conrad, whose imagination was already sparking ideas. "Could be they just wanted to show us humans that they had the power to visit Earth whenever they wanted. Maybe they even dropped something on purpose to prove they were here."

His mind was racing ahead. "But if they did that, it couldn't have been very big because people on the Peak would have found it by now. So it must be just tiny bits. Things so hard to find, only earthlings with imaginations as good as theirs could find them."

"Earthlings like us, Conrad," said Nico.

"Yeah, exactly like us. Team, we've gotta check this out."

When the boys got to class, everyone was talking about what their parents had seen. They were so excited that their teacher thought it would be a perfect time for an astronomy lesson.

The class listened with interest as she described the many different kinds of objects that are sometimes seen in the night sky.

Greg Berman was eager to share what he learned when he visited a planetarium in New York City. "A fireball is a meteor brighter than the planet Venus," he proudly explained.

Harry told them about a meteor war he had read about in his favourite graphic comic By the end of the discussion, most of the kids agreed that what the adults had seen was either a comet or some other combination of space rocks, iron, and frozen gases.

But not Conrad. No, he wasn't so easily persuaded.

In the carpool going home, Conrad revealed his latest plan.

"School's closed tomorrow for the Chung Yeung Festival but lucky for us our ancestors aren't buried here, so we don't have to spend the holiday sweeping stuff off their graves. We're free to do what we want. And I vote we go to the Peak and check things out for ourselves. If we can find proof that the aliens were here, boy, would that surprise everybody."

"Dad, I vote with Conrad. I'd rather go exploring than fly kites like the rest of the kids do during the festival. Would you drive us to the Peak tomorrow?" asked Nico.

"Certainly. If that's what you boys prefer, it's fine with me. But don't get your hopes up. You might be very disappointed when you can't find what you're looking for."

Bright and early the next morning, Conrad rummaged through his collector's drawer. He took out his magnifying glass, his poking stick, and a flashlight. Then he sat back on his heels to think. After all, he had never been on a hunt for alien droplets before and he wanted to be sure he'd have everything he might need. He searched through his expedition stuff one last time before deciding to play it safe by taking everything just in case.

As promised, Mr. Daniels drove the boys to the Peak. "I'll be back at two o'clock. That should give you enough time," he said as the three friends got out of the car.

Usually Conrad began to search as soon as he arrived at his destination. But not this time. This time he stood as still as a spider waiting for an insect to enter its web. He was concentrating as hard as he could, trying to imagine where he would have dropped something if he were an extraterrestrial creature who wanted to leave proof of his visit.

The boys waited quietly. They knew not to disturb Conrad when he was thinking

Finally, Conrad said, "This isn't going to be an easy expedition, team. There are houses everywhere. We have to hunt on people's property."

"Won't we need permission?" asked the ever-so-polite Nico.

"We can't wait for permission. Anyway, the people won't know 'cause they'll be away taking care of their dead ancestors' graves. It's actually a perfect time."

Conrad led the boys around the back of a huge red house. They searched and searched. They found various coloured rocks, an icky piece of used dental floss, and a squashed tin of Liang Cha tea but nothing that looked like it could have dropped from a spaceship.

Next they went into the garden behind a grey and white stone house. They searched and searched. Once again, they didn't find anything unusual.

"Do you think our teacher was right? Maybe it was only a comet or a meteor," suggested Nico, who was getting discouraged.

"No way. It had to be a spaceship. We just aren't looking in the right place. That's all," said Conrad, sounding so sure of himself that the others thought he must be right.

The three of them were bent over, searching the ground in the next garden, when they heard shouting. "What are you whippersnappers doing in my garden?" yelled an old man. "Go fly your kites somewhere else.'"

"We aren't flying kites, sir," explained Conrad as the man approached, looking very angry indeed. "We're looking for evidence."

"Evidence? What kind of evidence?" the man asked in a voice louder than the boys liked to hear.

"Evidence that a spaceship was hovering over here last night."

"Oh, that kind of evidence," said the man, a smile changing his once grumpy-looking face. "Why didn't you say so? Good luck to you, lads, but mind, don't trample on any flowers."

The boys were about to enter the back-yard of the next house when they heard loud growling.

"There's a dog there. I don't want to go where there's a dog," said Aidan.

Neither did the older boys, so they ran past that house.

"Maybe we got it wrong. Maybe the aliens knew we'd get into trouble if went exploring in people's backyards. Maybe they dropped their evidence in front of the houses to make it a bit easier. Let's check out that flowerbed over there."

Off the boys went. Once again Conrad, magnifying glass in hand, began to search. And search. And search. Suddenly he spied something.

"Quick, team. Over here. You've gotta see this." He held up a thin wire that was twisted round and round. It had tiny, springy parts jutting out of both ends.

"Nix-nix chopsticks. That's just a rusty old coil," said Nico, looking at the small, spring-like object. "It could have come from anything."

"It did come from anything. An alien any-thing. This has to be part of an antenna from a UFO. Everybody knows UFOs need super-sonic radar equipment with antennas to guide them through space," said Conrad as he care-fully wrapped up his latest treasure and slipped it into his sample bag. "I think we're finally in the right spot."

The boys continued their search. It was hard work. They found some funny-shaped rocks that Aidan thought the aliens might have dropped. The older boys didn't think they were space rocks, but they let Aidan believe what he wanted.

They found a tans piece which had gone missing from a child's tangram puzzle, and a broken tile from a mahjong set. Nico found a thick piece of glass, but even using their imaginations, they didn't think it was from a spaceship. It looked too much like part of a Coke bottle.

It was getting late. Nico and Aidan were ready to call it quits. It hadn't been a very exciting adventure, and Nico was about to tell Conrad they wanted to go home when they heard him shout, "Over here, team. You won't believe what I just found."

The boys rushed toward Conrad. He was bent over, examining a green jellybean-looking blob that was stuck to the side of a path leading to the house.

"This is from an alien's body. I've seen pictures of them in books. They're almost always green and shiny like this," said Conrad, carefully scraping the blob off the walk as he continued to explain.

"Aliens aren't like us. They're much, much smarter. I'll bet they can even grow extra body parts. That way they can release small pieces of themselves whenever they want to prove to us earthlings that they exist."

"Fantastico," said Nico. "It makes sense. If they come all the way from other planets, for sure they can do all kinds of cool things like making extra body parts."

"Can I smell it?" asked Aidan.

The older boys smiled. They didn't get why Aidan wanted to smell strange things, but they were feeling pretty good about their find and saw no reason not to agree.

"Sure, kid," said Conrad holding the greenish blob towards Aidan, who leaned in for a whiff.

"Smells like an alien body part to me," said Aidan.

That being confirmed, the boys high-fived each other.

"We did it, team. We found evidence proving space creatures were here," said Conrad.

Just then, Mr. Daniels arrived. Instead of the three sad and disappointed-looking boys he had expected to take home, he was greeted by three smiling collectors.

"We got it, Dad. We found evidence that aliens were really here," said Nico.

Mr. Daniels looked at the three delighted boys. He wasn't convinced the evidence would check out, but he knew that didn't really matter.

What mattered most was the boys had used their imaginations. And imagination, as everyone knows, is the most important part of any expedition.

Something to think about my
Fellow Adventurers:

Though something starts in a clever way
it may not turn out right.
Like when Conrad looked in the mirror
and gave himself a fright.
You may find it funny
it wasn't Conrad at his best
but it did take imagination
for that he passed the test.

CHAPTER EIGHT

CATS WHISKERS AND OTHER HAIRY THINGS

It was April, the start of Hong Kong's rainy season. Conrad hated the rainy season. He hated seeing the ugly grey sky. He hated hearing the rain pounding against the windows. Most of all, he hated having to stay indoors.

"I'm a collector. Everybody knows that collectors need to go on expeditions to get the best stuff. There isn't anything good to collect when I'm stuck in the house," Conrad muttered to himself.

But there was no going outside that day. A typhoon, with winds strong enough to uproot trees, strong enough to blow young children and old ladies right off their feet, was raging outside.

Conrad put his head in his hands and concentrated. "Think, Conrad. Think. There has to be something interesting in this house that I never thought to collect before," he said.

Conrad was an excellent thinker. It was how he made his imagination work, and Conrad was happiest when his imagination was working. Even though at times his thinking got him into trouble.

When he was in school, the teacher would scold, "Conrad, we need your mind here in the class, not off goodness knows where."

Other times, when he'd be thinking very hard, trying to get his imagination sparking, his mother would snap, "Stop your daydreaming, Conrad. You need to pay attention when I'm talking to you."

Conrad knew that grown-ups didn't understand how important it was that he concentrate, especially when he had that jumpy, tingling, not-to-be-denied feeling like he had today.

I've got to collect something. I've just got to.
He felt the sparks swimming round and round
in his mind.

At times like this, Conrad would wonder why
he couldn't be like everyone else and be happy
collecting baseball cards or stuff like that. But
those thoughts only lasted a moment or so,
and then he'd be back challenging his imagination to come up with something, anything,
that was cool and out of the ordinary.

"The scabs were sooooo perfect. I didn't
have to go out in the rain to get them. The
collection just grew itself wherever I was …
wait a minute. If scabs worked well, other
body parts could too. Why didn't I think of
that before!" he said.

Conrad rushed into his room and headed
straight for the drawer where he kept his
expedition equipment. He took out a pair
of scissors, a magnifying glass, and some

plastic baggies. From there he headed to the bathroom.

Conrad looked at himself in the mirror. He looked at his hair. It was rather ordinary. *Nothing interesting there,* he thought.

He looked at his eyelashes. They were long. Conrad thought they were much too long. People were always saying, "Oh, Conrad, what beautiful lashes you have. They're so long and silky-looking. They belong on a girl."

Conrad thought that was a very dumb thing to say.

"Girl lashes that come from a boy, now that's different enough to be part of a collection," he said.

Taking up his scissors, he snipped off his lashes and put them carefully into a plastic baggy.

Conrad stared at the space where his eyelashes had been. His eyelids looked weird.

"Nobody can say that I have girl lashes now. They can't even say that I have boy lashes. My eyes look bald! If Mom sees this, she'll kill me."

Conrad raced back into his room and opened his collector's drawer once again. He took out a pair of sunglasses and put them on. Even though he was in the house. Even though it was a dull, rainy day.

"The lashes are a start, but I need to collect a lot more hairs if this is to become an honest-to-goodness collection. Could be there's something interesting in Mom and Dad's room."

Conrad grabbed his magnifying glass and slipped unnoticed into his parents' bedroom. Slowly and carefully, he checked out the bed, the floor, and the closet. He found a few hairs lying about but nothing special. Certainly nothing unusual enough to add to his collection.

Conrad thought some more. *There's always that stupid-looking tied-up spritz of hair that sticks up from Suzy's head. Mommy says she puts the ribbon around it so that the hair won't fall in Suzy's eyes. I could cut the spritz off and save Mom the trouble. Nah, she would probably freak out, and even if she didn't, what's so cool about having a collection of baby curls?*

Conrad's thoughts were interrupted by Mewsy, the family's playful Siamese cat. Mewsy had a knack for sneaking up on anyone who seemed to be deep in thought and pouncing on them.

Today was no exception. As Conrad sat pondering his next move, Mewsy crept up until she was just inches from his face and let out a loud, high-pitched Siamese meow. Conrad looked at his pet. He saw a wide-open mouth, perky brown ears, and quivering white whiskers.

"Whiskers of a cat. Purr ... fect," said Conrad. Without missing a beat, he swooped down and picked up his little pal. Zip. Before Mewsy could mew in protest, Conrad snipped off almost all of the whiskers on one side of her face. He was about to even out her new look when zap! Mewsy twisted, squirmed, jumped from his grasp, and disappeared underneath the hall table.

Ever so carefully, Conrad put the white cat whiskers into a plastic baggy.

His next stop was the living room. He was so engrossed in his hunt that at first he didn't notice his grandpa, who was visiting from Montreal, sitting in the corner chair near the fireplace. Conrad wasn't sure if Grandpa was asleep or merely resting his eyes, so he approached him quietly.

That's when he saw it!

It was black. It was straight. It was the most humongous nose hair Conrad had ever seen, and it was pointing right at him. It seemed to be saying, "Look at me, Conrad. You couldn't ask for a better specimen than me."

Conrad lost no time. He was glad that he had his own scissors. No way could he have used the huge pair his mother kept in the kitchen. After all, he didn't want to cut off Grandpa's nose just to get a hair for his collection.

Conrad took off his sunglasses. He carefully leaned over Grandpa. Just as he was about to cut the nose hair, Grandpa gave a mighty snore. The nose hair quivered, then poof! It shot right back up into Grandpa's nose.

Before Conrad could say "wo-bah," which is what he often said when he was dreadfully disappointed, Grandpa snorted, and out popped the nose hair. Just as black. Just as straight. Pointed once again in the direction of Conrad.

Before Grandpa had time to take another breath, Conrad reached down. Zip! Off came the hair. Then zap. Horror of horrors, the hair fell from the nose and disappeared.

Conrad looked down the front of Grandpa's shirt. He didn't see it. What he did see was Grandpa staring down at him.

"And what might you be doing, young man?" asked Grandpa.

"I-I-I was just looking for something, Grandpa."

"And I suppose what you're looking for needs cutting?" asked Grandpa, looking at the scissors in Conrad's hand. Before Conrad could answer, Grandpa shifted in the chair.

"Don't get up, Grandpa. I'll never find it if you stand up."

"Find what? What could you possibly be looking for?"

"Your nose hair, Grandpa."

"My..." Before Grandpa could finish the sentence, Conrad reached over and pinched Grandpa's arm. "Conrad, what has gotten into you today?"

"Look, Grandpa. I got it. It was on your arm. See? Isn't it cool?" said Conrad, proudly holding up the blackest, tiniest hair imaginable.

But Grandpa wasn't interested in the rescued nose hair. He was looking directly at Conrad, and he couldn't quite believe what he saw.

"Conrad, what happened to your eyes? My goodness, boy, what have you done to yourself?"

Conrad was so pleased to have recovered the nose hair, he had forgotten about his bald eyelids. Slowly, he looked up at his Grandpa. He knew he didn't have a choice. He had to tell his grandfather about his latest collection. So he did.

When he was through, Grandpa broke into a hearty laugh. "That's some hunt you're on, my lad. Boy's silky lashes, whiskers of a cat, nose hair from an old man. Sounds like you're preparing a witch's brew more than putting together a collection."

"The trouble is this isn't working out the way I wanted, Grandpa. I don't like having bald eyes. Mewsy's hiding under the hall table and won't come out, and cutting off nose hairs, especially when someone is snoring, is pretty gross. I'm going to stop this and stick to having just one body part collection."

"One body part collection! You mean to say you have another one?"

"Uh, we can't talk about that now, Grandpa. The typhoon has passed. It's hardly raining anymore. I'm going over to Nico and Aidan's house. Even if this didn't turn out to be one of my best collections, I still don't want these tiny hairs to get lost before they've had a chance to see them."

With that Conrad slipped his sunglasses back on and headed out into the dull, rainy April day.

**Can you imagine what it's like
to work as hard as hard can be
only to have your collection
get sent across the sea?
That is what Conrad did face
in the chapter just ahead
and sadly, it wasn't his imagination
that filled him full of dread.**

CHAPTER NINE

THE BIG, DISASTROUS MOVE

Conrad was so excited he forgot to put his underwear on when he dressed that morning. So excited that when he went to feed his pets, he put the birdseed in the turtle bowl and the fish food in his little sister's cereal bowl.

Yes, Conrad was excited all right, because in just a few days the movers were coming and the family would be on their way to New York City. Conrad had loved living in Hong Kong, but still, he was happy the bank was sending them back to their own country, even though it meant he wouldn't be an expat explorer any longer.

His dad had told him about all the fun things New York had to offer. He couldn't wait to roller-blade in Central Park, go to real grown-up pro baseball games, and explore the *Intrepid*, the huge battleship that was docked in the New York harbour.

It's going to be excellent, Conrad told himself as he carefully continued to pack his collections into the large carton his mother had given him. But inside, way deep down inside, he was worried. Worried because he was leaving Nico and Aidan, his best expedition buddies and didn't know if he'd find friends in New York that would be as much fun to go collecting with as those two were.

And most of all, he worried that his collections might get lost during the move.

"If my collections get lost, I'll die. I'll just lie down and die," Conrad moaned.

"What makes you think you're going to die?" asked his mother, who had come into the room with yet another box in her hands.

"I was thinking about my collections and the movers," said Conrad. "What if they don't take care of my collections properly? What if my box gets lost? What if someone steals it?"

The more "what ifs" Conrad thought of, the more worried he became.

"Remember what I told you about 'what ifs,' Connie?"

"Yeah, I know." He recited the little verse his mother always told him when he started to imagine bad things happening.

The worry bug gets a whiff

Each time we say "What if?"

"What if?" makes him move in close

And spray us with his worry dose.

"You got it." laughed his mother. "'What ifs' can get real scary if you let them run free in your imagination."

"Can you promise my collection won't get lost?" asked Conrad, who by now was so full of his "what ifs" that he had worried himself silly.

"I promise," said his mother, who was certain his collections would arrive safely.

Unfortunately, she was very much mistaken.

The family arrived in New York at the end of August. Two days later, their furniture and boxes arrived. That is, all their furniture and most of their boxes arrived.

One large box was missing. Conrad's box with all his precious collections didn't arrive with the others. His wonderful treasures were gone!

"It's just not possible," said Conrad's mother.

"It's unthinkable," said Conrad's dad.

Even Conrad's little sister, Suzy, who still wasn't too sure where she was, knew something was amiss.

"Is it possible we could we have forgotten to put the address on that box?" Conrad's dad wondered aloud.

"Of course not. I glued the label on myself," replied Conrad's mother.

"And I wrote 'Collections' all over the box, on every side and on the top," said Conrad.

He was fighting back tears, but it looked like he was going to lose the battle at any moment.

"Don't you worry, son," said his dad, feeling almost as bad as Conrad did. "I'll get this straightened out. You'll have that box in just a day or so."

Conrad believed his father could do almost anything. So with hope in his heart, he waited for a delivery van to come. He waited and he waited. He waited all the following morning and afternoon. He waited all the next day and the day after that. A whole week passed and still no box. He waited until it was September and it was time to start school.

As expected, the first day was difficult. Conrad felt uncomfortable, even shy, and shy was a brand-new feeling for Conrad. He looked over at the kids in his class. They looked friendly enough. Conrad knew that somewhere in that group of children there was one, maybe two who in time would become his new best friends. But it was too early to tell who they might be.

Before the lesson started, the teacher introduced Conrad to the class. "Conrad, would you like to tell the class a bit about yourself?" she asked.

What can I say? Conrad thought. *I can't tell them I'm a collector. They'll want to see what I've collected, and I have nothing to show them.*

So instead Conrad simply told the class that he had been an expat living in Hong Kong. The kids found that very interesting. They had many questions. They were curious as to what he had done there.

Conrad told them about his rides on junks and longboats. He told them about the day trip he took on a hydrofoil to see thousands of Terracotta Warriors that had once been buried alongside an emperor who believed they'd protect him in his afterlife. He told his new classmates that he had seen giant panda bears, ridden an elephant and once had a man wrap a python around his neck. He told them lots of things, but he didn't tell them how much he loved collecting stuff. Not one word.

Before he realized it, two more weeks had passed and still no collection.

His father had called the moving company. His mother had called the moving company. The only thing the moving company could tell them was that all their boxes had been placed in a large wooden crate and shipped directly to New York. Once the ship arrived, all the crates were unloaded and opened and all the individual boxes were delivered to where they were supposed to go.

"Where that one box ended up is anybody's guess," they told Conrad's parents.

Conrad's mother felt terrible. Conrad's father was very upset. But no one, absolutely no one, felt worse than Conrad did. His life's work was missing!

Oh, how he wished that they had never left Hong Kong.

Days passed. Conrad became more and more comfortable with the kids at school. He was beginning to think that Jamie might become his new best friend, maybe not as good a friend as Nico, but a good best friend anyway. Actually, Conrad was thinking just that when the teacher called for everybody's attention.

"Boys and girls, I have a special treat for you today. We're going on a field trip to the museum. There's a special exhibition that I think you'll enjoy. It's called Hobbies and the World's Children.

"A hobby," Ms. Roth went on to explain, "is something people do in their spare time for their own enjoyment."

"I know," said Brian. "I have a hobby. I make model airplanes."

"I collect stamps," said Cindy.

"I paint. Yes indeedy, painting's my hobby," Melinda chimed in.

Conrad didn't say a word.

"Well, I'll give everyone a chance to tell us about their own hobbies after we see the exhibition. Right now we have to get our jackets and get going."

The children raced excitedly to the locker room. All, that is, except Conrad.

"Come on, Connie," yelled Jamie. "Hurry up."

Conrad couldn't get the teacher's words out of his ears.

Conrad didn't want to go to the exhibition. He didn't want to see other kids' hobbies or hear about them either, and most of all he didn't want to talk about his hobby.

However, once they were actually at the exhibition, Conrad's attitude began to improve. After all, he was a curious boy. He was interested in other kids and what they liked to do, especially kids from other lands. By the time the teacher divided the class into two groups, Conrad, though not happy, was in a better mood.

Ms. Roth took some of the children off to the North Room, while Conrad and his about-to-become new best friend, Jamie, and Pierce, who was also becoming a best friend, and some other kids went to the South Room with Mrs. Golden, Carol's mom, who was the teacher's helper that day.

The children saw all kinds of interesting things that girls and boys from different countries had made. There was a tea doll from

Labrador, rag balls from Peru, and colourful beaded bracelets made by a young girl in Mexico. There were photographs of children doing science experiments, others with binoculars birdwatching, and some were fly fishing, which the boys thought looked especially cool.

Despite himself, Conrad was becoming more interested.

Then it was time for the two groups to switch rooms. "Wait till you see the wishing dolls a girl in Guatemala made," said Carrie, a girl from Conrad's group, to Danielle as the two groups were passing each other in the hallway.

"You won't believe the stuff some guy collected," Leon whispered to Conrad and Jamie.

"Yeah, it's wild!" said Mitchell.

Conrad's heart sank again. *I don't want to see someone else's collection. I want to see mine.* Tears filled his eyes, and only because he desperately didn't want to cry in front of the other kids was he able to blink them away.

The North Room was set up very much like the south one. There were photos on the walls showing children doing many interesting things. Some were flying kites. Others, dressed in colourful costumes, were dancing. One boy looked like he was trying to milk a camel but that wasn't for sure. Most interesting were the large glass cases scattered throughout the room filled with things the children had made.

The kids ran off in all directions. Lewis Yaffe, who was the most adventurous of the lot, raced to the far end of the room. He peered into a case for just a second or two before spinning around.

"Hey, Jamie. Quick, come here. You've gotta see this. It's soooo cool."

Jamie hurried over. Conrad followed more slowly. "It's some kid's collection. You won't believe what he's found."

"Wow," said Jamie. "Look at this. The note says it's pirate stuff. There's even a bone from a pirate's parrot."

"Hey, guys, this has gotta be the best ever. This guy even collected scabs."

"Gross," said the two cousins, Ella and Simone, in unison.

"What do you girls know," said Pierce, who didn't think a scab collection was at all gross.

"Look at the alien part. Is this guy ever lucky. I wish I could find something from an alien," said Lewis, who loved everything to do with space.

By this time, all the kids had gathered around the case. Everyone was talking at once as they excitedly pointed out the various objects.

Only one person was completely silent. As you may have guessed, that was Conrad. He was too shocked to say a word. Too stunned to even move. For there in front of him, at this important exhibition of Hobbies of the World's Children, was his very own collection.

"Look. It says that it was collected by Unknown in Hong Kong," said Ellie.

"He's not called Unknown, silly," said Robert. "That means that they don't know the name of the person, that's all."

"Then how do they know where he lived, big shot?" said Ellie. She wasn't going to let anyone get away with calling her silly.

"That's a very good question," said Mrs. Golden. "But we need to move on. There's still more to see, and it will soon be time to leave."

Reluctantly, the children started to move away, but not Conrad. He just stood silently peering into the case in front him.

"Come on now, Conrad," Mrs. Golden urged. "You'll miss the rest of the exhibition."

Still, he couldn't move a muscle. It was as if Conrad himself had become one of the statues in the museum.

Mrs. Golden sensed something wasn't quite right. She went over to Conrad and lightly touched his shoulder. That gentle touch seemed to release something that had been caught up inside him.

Conrad started jumping up and down, pointing, and saying, "It's mine. It's my collection. Hey, everybody, I'm Unknown. I'm the collector."

He was so excited and so proud and so happy that his words fell all over themselves. No one, not even Ms. Golden, was certain of what he was saying.

"Slow down, Conrad," she said. "Are you telling us that you collected all these wonderful things?"

"Yes, you see, I packed my things in a big box and I wrote 'Collection' and ... and..."

The children, sensing something was happening, had gathered around Conrad.

He explained everything. How right from the beginning he was scared that it might get lost. How he had written 'Collection' all over the box. How his dad was told the crate had arrived at the dock, and how the box with his collection had mysteriously disappeared.

By the time he finished, Ms. Roth and the other group of children had come into the North Room. They saw the children crowded together around one case, and Ms. Roth called from the entranceway, "Everyone, it's time to leave. The bus is outside waiting to take us back to class."

"It looks like we have a bit of an emergency here," explained Mrs. Golden.

The children, led by Ms. Roth, hurried over to where Conrad and his group had gathered. Conrad repeated what he had just discovered to his teacher and the second group of kids.

"We must report this to the museum officials right away," said Ms. Roth.

While they waited for the curator of the exhibition to come down from his office, a very happy Conrad told his classmates all about the adventures he and his friends, Nico and Aidan, had collecting the pirate stuff. He told them about the problems they had encountered on the Peak and how they managed to eat the cookie collection and keep it at the same time.

But he didn't tell them about the time long ago when he tried to collect icicles and lumps of snow. That would remain his and his grand-ma's secret forever.

Conrad told his story one more time to Mr. Whitehouse, the museum's curator.

"That explains it," Mr. Whitehouse said when Conrad was finished. "The people at the docks knew about our exhibition. They had been delivering the things that you see here for weeks. Crates and boxes were shipped from all around the world. When the shipment arrived from Hong Kong, one of the boxes had 'Collections' written all over it, but there was no address. The label must have fallen off. So the handlers at the dock just figured it was being shipped to us for the exhibition.

"I am really sorry, Conrad. It must have been awful for you to think your collection was lost all this time. But I must admit that I am happy for the museum that it arrived here. As you can see, it is one of the most interesting hobbies we have on exhibition. You sure are a fine collector."

Upon hearing the curator's words, Conrad's classmates all began to clap and cheer.

The very next day, at the special invitation of the curator, Conrad returned to the museum with his mother, father, and Suzy. They headed straight for the case that housed Conrad's exhibit. There, in the corner of the right-hand side, just as the curator had promised, was a sign reading "Collection by Conrad 'the Collector' Vosko. Formerly of Hong Kong, now residing in New York."

Conrad stared at the sign for a long time. He felt so good. So very, very good.

He knew he was going to love New York.

Conrad's adventures have come to an end,

but worry not,

my adventurous friend.

If you read them again,

you can still enjoy

the collecting adventures

of this awesome boy.

Printed in May 2019
by Rotomail Italia S.p.A., Vignate (MI) - Italy